My Mom Hates Me in January

Judy Delton

Pictures by **John Faulkner**

Albert Whitman & Company, Chicago

For Jamie Delton—
whose mother hates him in January
but loves him the other twelve months
of the year.

Library of Congress Cataloging in Publication Data

Delton, Judy

My mom hates me in January.
SUMMARY: A little boy finds it is the winter blues
and not his behavior that makes his mother impatient in
January.
[1. Mothers and sons—Fiction. 2. Winter—Fiction]
I. Faulkner, John Frink II. Title.
PZ7.D388My   [E]   77-5749
ISBN 0-8075-5356-5

12   11   10   9   8   7   6   5

About This Story . . .

In picture book stories, parents are often understanding, happy, and generous, even in the face of outrageous behavior exhibited by their children. But girls and boys may be pardoned if they look with some doubt at these happy families living and meeting problems together.

The truth is that parents are human beings and have a full range of feelings, and these include anger, depression, and impatience. In this story, it's Lee Henry's mother rather than Lee Henry who has a problem, a familiar one. January is a depressing month to face, and nothing seems right. Lee Henry copes with his mother's mood as best he can and realizes in his own way that his mother's feelings really have little to do with him. He finds out, too, that a difficult mood doesn't last forever and that smiles and happiness return. It's a welcome, reassuring discovery anyone who enjoys Lee Henry's story can share.

My mom hates me
in January.
She says spring
will never come.
She says if winter
doesn't end
in five minutes
she'll have a
nervous breakdown.

"Get that clay out of the living room,"
she says.
"Get that dog out of the kitchen,
Lee Henry!"

"Why are you always
under my feet?"
my mother asks.

I want to play monsters,
but it's too noisy.

I want to make popcorn balls,
but it's too messy.
I want Mom to read a book to me,
but she's too busy.
"Winter is getting awfully long,
Lee Henry," she tells me.
"Get dressed and go outside."

I put my snowsuit on backwards.
I put my boots on the wrong feet.
I put my cap on inside out.
I tie my scarf around my neck too tight.
My mittens feel wet inside.

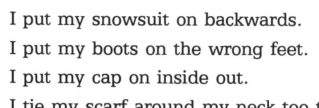

"Good heavens, Lee Henry!"
says my mother.
"Can't you do anything alone?"

Mom puts my snowsuit on frontwards.
She puts my boots on the other feet.
She turns my cap right side out.
She ties my scarf loose
and gives me dry mittens.

"Have a good time, Lee Henry.
Don't go in the street
or lose your mittens.
Don't put snow in your mouth
or get snow inside your boots.
Keep dry and don't slide into a tree."

I call for George,
but he is in school.
I slide on my saucer
and just miss a tree.

I make a snowman, but his head falls off.
I make angels in the snow and get wet
to my underwear.

On the way to shoveling the sidewalk
I lose a mitten.

"I am going in," I say to no one.
No one answers.

"Lee Henry,
are you coming in
already?
You just went out.
Don't track up
the kitchen floor
with those wet boots,"
my mom says.

I put my snowsuit on the radiator.
I shake the snow out of my boots
and put them in the basement.
I put my scarf and one mitten
on the closet shelf.
Then I sneeze.

"Lee Henry, are you getting
another cold?"
says my mother.
"Take a warm bath."

When I take my bath,
Mom says I splash on the floor.
When I take my nap,
Mom says I jump on the bed.

When I eat dinner,
she says,
"Don't tip on that chair,
Lee Henry!"

"If winter lasts
   five minutes more,
   I am going to have
   a nervous breakdown,"
   I say to no one.

No one answers.

I put on my warm pajamas
and crawl in bed.

The next morning
at breakfast,
my mother says,
"Look! What is that
beside the fence?"

We go to the window.
We look at something
red and brown in the snow.
"Lee Henry!" shouts my mother.
"I do believe it is a robin.
Spring is almost here!"

That afternoon we make popcorn balls
    (even if they're messy).
We make monsters out of clay in the living room
    (and Mom laughs).

I get my favorite book and Mom reads to me.
    (I sit on her lap.)
"What fun it will be when it is warm,"
she says.
"You will swim and ride your bike
and climb trees."
"I will play in the park with George
and build a treehouse," I say.

We go to the kitchen
and eat a popcorn ball
together
and drink a milkshake.
Even the dog has some.

My mom hates me in January
  (unless she just hates **January**).

But she'll love me again in May.